MARVEL

THOR™
THE DARK WORLD

THOR
THE DARK WORLD

Adapted by MICHAEL SIGLAIN

Based on the Screenplay by CHRISTOPHER L. YOST
and CHRISTOPHER MARKUS & STEPHEN McFEELY

Story by DON PAYNE and ROBERT RODAT

Produced by KEVIN FEIGE, p.g.a.

Directed by ALAN TAYLOR

New York • Los Angeles

Printed in the United States of America

First Edition

1 3 5 7 9 10 8 6 4 2

V475-2873-0-13227

ISBN 978-1-4231-7245-1

marvelbooks.com

SUSTAINABLE
FORESTRY
INITIATIVE

Certified Chain of Custody
Promoting Sustainable Forestry
www.sfiprogram.org
SFI-01054
The SFI label applies to the text stock

CONTENTS

PROLOGUE

BAM! The black-and-white soccer ball bounced down a flight of stairs, ricocheted off a nearby wall, then rocketed back toward the hard concrete steps. Racing down the staircase to catch up with the ball were two eight-year-old kids, Maddie and Navid. They were having the best time in the world, playing ball where they weren't supposed to, in an abandoned industrial complex on the south side of London. But nothing in the world could prepare them for what was about to happen next.

The soccer ball rolled back toward the first step, bounced, and then magically—unbelievably—rolled *up* the wall, defying gravity. Maddie and Navid stopped dead in their tracks. Did that just happen? They looked at each other in amazement. Smiles instantly stretched across their faces as the kids gave chase, more determined than ever to catch up with the magical ball.

As they ran down a long corridor, they passed yet another oddity: a window, with its glass seemingly broken and shattered, but somehow frozen in place. The kids looked closer and their smiles widened. In front of them were hundreds of shards of glass hanging in midair, as if by magic. A dripping sound then caught their attention, but when they searched for the puddle, they were shocked to see that it was above them. The water was dripping in *reverse*—down from the floor and up to the ceiling. All around them, oddities of unexplainable proportion unfolded before their very eyes. Astounded, the kids kept on chasing their ball.

Finally, Maddie and Navid located their ball in a large room. There, in the center of the room, was their soccer ball. But instead of lying on the floor, it was floating in midair, surrounded by dust and debris. As they entered, they felt a sudden charge of static electricity through the air, and the debris began to swirl. Navid grabbed the ball out of the air. He spun it in his hands for a few seconds, then smiled. Pulling back his arm he threw it as hard as he could. But before it could get farther than a few feet, the soccer ball simply disappeared. A moment later, the ball burst through a skylight, breaking the glass. The young children shielded their faces from the falling debris, but the shards of the skylight slowed and froze, like the window. Peeking through her fingers, Maddie gasped in delight and then belted out with laughter! Soon both kids were laughing until Maddie, eyes widened, pointed to Navid, as the boy's hair began to stand up on end. But the best part was yet to come. The children heard cranking and clinging coming from behind them. Racing to another larger, half-open room, they saw an old cement truck. But *this* cement truck was floating inches above the ground and slowly starting to rotate. Navid raced over to the truck and stopped inches from it, looking up at the massive piece of spinning, metal machinery. Then, he gently laid his fingers on the metal bumper and gave it a tiny push. The truck flew back and started to spin faster. Navid smiled a mischievous, happy grin at Maddie.

This was the start of something big. . . .

PART ONE

CHAPTER ONE

IN THE FAR reaches of space, light-years from Earth and the Milky Way galaxy, a dark planet rotated in silence, illuminated only by the sparkling stars that surrounded it. This was the planet Svartalfheim: once the home to a race of ancient Dark Elves, it was now a burned out, darkened husk of a world, barely even inhabitable. But that would soon change. . . .

As if by magic, or perhaps science, the stars around this desolate world began to warp and ripple as a large, ominous form emerged from the never-ending blackness of space. The stars gave light to this flying monstrosity and revealed its true form: a massive spacecraft, seemingly lifeless and adrift. But the closer it got to Svartalfheim, the more the ship began to come to life.

Ominous, black energy began to glow from the center of the ship, causing it to seem even more frightening and more intimidating than it already was. Inside this ship, which seemed more like a twisted haunted house in space than a high-tech spacecraft, a projection of a star map flickered to life. Inside a dark chamber, a countdown clock ticked toward zero.

Within the chamber, high above the floor, a large, dark figure hung from the ceiling. His arms wide, the elf was held suspended by tubes that were attached to his high-tech environment suit. The countdown ticked and ticked, closer and closer. And then finally it struck. Zero hour . . .

The Dark Elf's eyes opened with a start, their black centers a sign of keen determination, infinite sadness, and undiscovered cruelty. This was Malekith, leader of the Dark Elves of Svartalfheim.

Malekith descended to the floor, staggered, then slowly began to detach the support tubes. A strange ooze now flowed from the conduits onto the ground, spreading in every direction. His breathing shallow, the Dark Elf felt the air enter his lungs. Then, upon seeing his battle mask, he picked it up and regarded himself in its pearl-like reflection. Malekith was a horrifying vision: pale, with hairless skin and pointed ears. And his battle mask, with its featureless appearance, only made him more terrifying to behold.

Still holding on to the mask, Malekith slowly made his way to the ship's massive amphitheater. The Dark Elf peered out at the thousands of elves who were held there in suspended animation. They looked like six-foot, wingless, armored bats, all hanging perfectly still, just waiting for the call back to life, back to battle. But one other elf had already awoken: a large, muscled elf with a mask similar to Malekith's stood behind his leader. This was Algrim, Malekith's second in command.

"How many of us remain?" Malekith asked.

"Enough," replied Algrim, his head bowed slightly toward his master.

"Send out the scouts," Malekith commanded. "Let us see what has become of this poisoned universe."

Outside the ship, which was now crackling with more and more dark energy, small scout ships rocketed off in every direction. The Dark Elves had returned.

CHAPTER TWO

BEAUTIFUL golden sunlight shined down through the lush, vibrant forests of Vanaheim. Unlike Svartalfheim, the realm of Vanaheim was much more pleasant an environment. It was home to beautiful lakes and mountains, with vast fields of green spread out as far as the eye could see. But today, it was filled with danger and destruction.

The people of Vanaheim—known throughout the Nine Realms as the Vanir—raced through the forests as fast as they could. They were being chased by the Marauders, a race of space pirates—brutal invaders who were armed to the teeth and out for blood. Their sole purpose in life was to take what was not theirs, and destroy anything—and anyone—that stood in their way.

A frightened Vanir woman ran for her life but stumbled, falling down a riverbank just as a Marauder fired a massive fireball. It streaked above her head, impacting a nearby tree and causing it to burst into flames. As the woman regained her footing, she was confronted by a towering Marauder. He raised his razor-sharp ax, ready to strike, when suddenly a steel mace smashed the villain in the face, knocking him down, and knocking him out.

Standing over the frightened woman was her savior—Hogun the Grim, of the famous Warriors Three. Hogun did not wait for a thank you, nor did he want one. The Marauders were running rampant across his home world, and Hogun was determined to stop them.

As more Vanir ran to safety, Hogun stood his

ground—the only barrier between the fierce oncoming Marauders and the peaceful Vanir. The Asgardian warrior gripped his mace tightly and steeled himself, ready for what just might be the last battle of his life. With a skull-shattering roar, the Marauders charged, determined to crush Hogun, and the rest of the Vanir people.

The lead Marauder raised his broadsword and swung, but his blade was deflected by another sword—the sword belonging to Fandral the Dashing, the second member of the mighty Warriors Three! Fandral, still handsome as ever despite the battle, rode through the charging Marauders on his white horse, knocking down one intruder after another until he was able to make his way to Hogun, flashing a smile the entire way.

"Do we have a plan?" Fandral asked his fellow Warrior as he flipped the lead Marauder off his horse and tossed his broadsword to one of the Vanir guards.

"We stand and fight!" Hogun the Grim yelled.

Fandral rolled his eyes at his friend's single-minded determination to fight. Then a loud *Boom*, *Boom*, *Boom* echoed throughout the trees. Fandral, Hogun, and the rest of the Vanir stopped in their tracks and turned their attention toward the deafening noise. It was coming from beyond the woods, and whatever was making the noise was big. *Very* big. The ground shook and trees fell with each sound as the unseen threat got closer and closer. The Vanir did not follow Hogun's orders to stay and fight, but instead quickly retreated into the woods. The idea also crossed Fandral's mind.

"Have you considered 'turn and run'?" Fandral asked, but Hogun only frowned in response. Then the grim warrior looked up and over the tree line and began to back away as well. Finding a Marauder's horse without its rider, Hogun swung up into the saddle and galloped away. Fandral was close behind as explosions rang out throughout the woods. There would be time enough to fight later.

The two warriors quickly rode their horses into a clearing where the Marauders were fighting with a few of Asgard's elite guards, the Einherjar, who had come to help the Vanir. Hogun and Fandral stopped before one of their Asgardian compatriots, the strong and beautiful Lady Sif, who was just as brave and tough as the Warriors Three. Sif was on horseback, locked in furious battle with a dozen or so Marauders. Sif spun her bladed spear high over her head, taking down several of the barbarians, then split the spear in two, forming a magnificent blade for each hand. Sif fought with fierce determination against the horde, but despite her resolve, she was gravely outnumbered. With all her might, she flipped off of her horse and delivered a powerful kick to one of the Marauders, sending him flying back past the third member of the Warriors Three, Volstagg the Voluminous.

"Volstagg—on your left!" Sif cried. Without missing a beat, Volstagg swung his battle-ax at his attacker, striking him down with one fell swoop. And when another Marauder tried to attack him with a club, the voluminous one merely took the hit, then turned, broke the club in two, and backhanded the Marauder, sending him flying through the air. But all of this nonstop battling was beginning to take its toll on the excessively large warrior. Now out of breath, Volstagg made his way to a giant pile of timber where he could take a momentary break.

"What are you doing?" Sif yelled. She couldn't believe her eyes. Here they were in a heated battle with villains known for decimating anything in their path, and one of the legendary Warriors Three was taking a breather.

"Giving them a moment . . . to regroup . . . only fair . . ." Volstagg said between long, labored breaths. But no sooner did Volstagg stop to catch his breath than another horde of Marauders set their sights on the large warrior. They ran at him with their weapons drawn, but Volstagg merely kicked out the timber, causing it to collapse on and crush the approaching horde.

Volstagg gave himself a congratulatory grin, but it was short-lived, for just as he did, he was slashed across the back by a Marauder. He wasn't as unstoppable or impenetrable as he thought.

Nearby, Lady Sif wasn't faring too much better. She was surrounded, and a Marauder from across the battlefield was aiming his crossbow at her head.

Just as the snickering Marauder was about to squeeze the trigger, a huge thunderclap echoed throughout the land, and with a bright, blinding light, the Bifrost—the way in which Asgardians traveled between the realms—fired down from the heavens into the center of the battlefield—and directly on top of the Marauder with the crossbow. Lady Sif raised her arm to shield her eyes from the spectacular blinding light and was just barely able to make out two Einherjar on horseback bursting from the glowing white column and charging into battle. One of the Marauders used this commotion to sneak up behind Volstagg. He raised his sword high above his head, preparing to strike down the warrior, when a whizzing sound echoed from within the Bifrost. As the light died down and the smoke began to clear, the sound intensified. Suddenly, an object rocketed out of the Bifrost, sliced across the battlefield at supersonic speed, and slammed into its target: the Marauder who was about to strike down Volstagg. The Marauder flew through the air and kept on flying. And flying. Volstagg turned, and upon investigation made out the object that had saved his life. It was the most famous weapon in all the Nine Realms. It was Mjolnir.

The powerful hammer, which was forged in the heart of a dying star and used by only he who is worthy, hovered in midair before speeding back across the battlefield to the hand of its wielder—the mighty Thor!

Thor, Prince of Asgard and son of Odin Allfather, emerged from the light of the Bifrost looking battle-worn but still majestic, and the sight of him instantly gave the Warriors Three, the Einherjar, and the Vanir a renewed sense of hope. Now that Thor was here, they were sure to defeat the Marauders. But Lady Sif felt that she didn't need Thor's help to win the day.

"Shouldn't you be battling trolls in Nornheim?" Sif said with a scowl.

"I ran out of trolls," Thor said with a charming smile. "Heimdall said these Marauders were giving you trouble," he added.

"I have this completely under control," Sif retorted.

Thor surveyed the battlefield. "Is that why everything is on fire?"

"You think you can do better?" Sif challenged with a smile.

"It would be a challenge to do worse," Thor said dryly before being surprise-attacked by two extra-big and extra-tough Marauders. Sif rolled her eyes in response, then joined her friend in battle.

Soon, Thor and Sif were joined by Fandral, Hogun, and Volstagg. As the battle raged on, Thor used Mjolnir to take out multiple Marauders at once. And when one Marauder thought he might be able to seize the hammer by grabbing on to it, the hammer simply pulled the invader through the air, right to Thor's waiting fist.

Thor, Lady Sif, and the Warriors Three fought bravely against the menacing Marauders, each one helping their fellow Asgardians. When one Marauder shot an arrow at Thor's head, Sif jumped into the air and raised her shield to block the attack. And when another fired a rocket launcher-like device, Thor valiantly deflected the blast with his mighty hammer, the impact from which knocked them all to the ground—hard.

As the Asgardians got back to their feet, they heard the same *Boom, Boom, Boom* sound that Fandral and Hogun had heard earlier. Whatever it was that was making that sound was much closer now. And the Marauders were getting ready for it. They parted the battlefield to make way, and the heroes looked up over the tree line and finally saw the cause of the sound.

A giant Kronan stone monster, made entirely of rock and standing fifteen feet tall, loomed before Thor and the Warriors Three. He held a massive metal club and looked down upon the Asgardians with contempt. The monster was about to crush their bones into dust.

"All yours," Sif said to Thor as she and the Warriors Three began to back away. The Marauders cheered. This was the fight they had been waiting for! Surely nothing could stop their stone man, not even the Mighty Thor. The rock monster smashed his club into the ground and let out a thunderous roar, signaling the start of the battle.

"I accept your surrender," Thor said, but the monster only raised its club higher, preparing to strike. But Thor was ready. Holding Mjolnir by the strap, Thor began to spin his hammer. It spun faster and faster and faster until it was nothing but a blur and Thor was rocketed off the ground in flight. The monster roared again as Thor, flying with his arm outstretched and all the might of Mjolnir in front of him, launched himself directly at the great beast. There was a deafening *CHOOM* as the hammer connected with the creature, then a blinding explosion. The Marauders looked up in disbelief and their cheering stopped. Chunks of rock rained from the sky as the monster's feet stumbled backward, disconnected to its body, which no longer existed. The upper half of the stone man had been completely obliterated by Thor.

The Son of Odin gripped Mjolnir tightly and turned with a scowl toward the rest of the Marauders. Almost in union, the remaining Marauders dropped their weapons and raised their hands in surrender. The battle was over.

"Next time we should just start with the big one," Fandral said with a smile.

In the aftermath of the battle, the Marauders had all been shackled together and lined up for their trip back to Asgard, and to prison. Escorted by the Einherjar, they made their way over to where Heimdall would open the Bifrost. All the while the Vanir watched, thankful that their realm was now free from danger. The Vanir sighed. Yes, their campground and village had been destroyed and mostly burned down in the fierce battle, but they would rebuild. They were a strong race, and this is what made them a part of the Nine Realms.

Hogun the Grim was talking to a Vanir woman

and her child, but broke off his conversation to rejoin Thor. "I am ready," the warrior said, his mace at his side.

"No," Thor began, as he gently placed his hand on the warrior's chest. "The peace is nearly won across the Nine Realms. It's best to be where your heart is. For now, Asgard can wait."

Hogun clenched his black mace. He wanted Thor to know that this was his battle just as much as it was Thor's. He wanted Thor to know that he would fight till the end to bring peace, not only to Vanaheim, but to the Nine Realms. Yet Hogun didn't have to say this. After years of battling monsters, Frost Giants, and ungodly beasts, these two friends had an unspoken bond. Thor knew how Hogun felt. And Thor also knew that Hogun had a family to watch over. Hogun closed his eyes and sighed, then looked over at his family. Thor was right.

Hogun the Grim nodded to the Mighty Thor, grateful and thankful for his old friend's compassion.

If it wasn't for Thor, Hogun's people and family would not be here. "You have my thanks," Hogun said as the two clasped wrists.

"And you, mine," Thor said as Hogun returned to his hillside ridge and his wife and child.

Thor looked to the bright, blue skies to signal the keeper of the Bifrost, the all-seeing, all-knowing sentry Heimdall. "Heimdall, when you are ready!" But as the Bifrost blasted down from the sky and transported everyone back to Asgard, two Marauders, who were hiding behind a ridge, saw this opportunity as their chance to escape. They ran back into the forest, but soon came face-to-face with two beings that they did not recognize. They were Dark Elf Scouts.

The two scouts stood firm, their masks expressionless. The Marauders, too, stood, unsure what to make of the situation. One Marauder began to move, but one of the Dark Elves tilted his head just a bit. It was just enough. The Dark Elf held up an over-sized rifle-like device and pointed it at one of the

Marauders. The space pirate's eyes grew wide with fear, and before he could react, two tiny projectiles fired out, eventually touching one another. The dark matter then created a tiny black hole. It floated over to the Marauder and sucked his body inside, imploding on itself.

The second Marauder merely watched in horror, frozen in fear by what had just happened. His mouth quivered. What were these menacing beings? What form of magic was this? Was he next? The Marauder began to back away, but it was no use. The Dark Elf fired his black energy gun right at him, and he, too, was sucked into the black hole, leaving only his horned helmet behind.

The Dark Elves looked from the ground to the bright light in the distance. With the Bifrost reflected in their helmet-covered eyes, they knew exactly what they had to report to Malekith.

CHAPTER THREE

IT WAS A TYPICALLY rainy day in London, and astrophysicist Jane Foster was nervous. She was running late for a meeting, but not one that had to do with science or what had happened a few years back in New Mexico. Nor was it anything S.H.I.E.L.D.-related. No, for Jane, this was much worse: Jane had a date.

Jane regarded herself in her bedroom mirror as she put on more eye shadow. Then, for the fourth time in five minutes, she brushed her brown hair. Then she fixed her shirt again. Then it was back to her hair. With a sigh, Jane finally gave in. She grabbed her jacket and made her way through her tiny flat to the door, passing a variety of scientific equipment along the way. As Jane slammed the door, she was unaware that one of her scanners had suddenly come to life and begun to go haywire.

Inside the Italian restaurant, Jane hid her face behind her menu, lifting it only slightly to peek across at her date, Richard, and give him a practiced smile. It was clear, at least to her, that she did not want to be there.

"The *osso buco* here is great," Richard said, trying to start some sort of conversation, but Jane just stared at him blankly. "On your profile it said you liked Italian," he continued, but again, Jane just stared back, expressionless. Richard sighed, put down the menu, and folded his hands on the table. "Someone else wrote your profile, didn't they?" he asked.

"How did you know?" Jane said, trying to make it seem like she really cared.

"Because when I asked you to dinner, you said

no, then yes, then yes but not now, then yes but not dinner, and now you've spent the first ten minutes of lunch studying a menu which only has three choices." Richard smiled. "Hence the *osso bucco*."

Jane gave him a warm, genuine smile. "It's complicated," she said, finally starting to open up.

"Is it another guy?" he asked.

"Sort of," Jane smiled. How could she tell him that the "other guy" was really Thor—Prince of Asgard, son of Odin Allfather, wielder of Mjolnir, and also a member of the Avengers?

"Is he still around?"

"No, he went away," Jane said with a slight sadness in her voice.

"Is he coming back?"

"I can't count on it," she said.

"Have you moved on?" Richard wondered.

"I'm . . . trying to," Jane said with all sincerity. Even though time had passed, she still wasn't over Thor. And she still missed him.

Richard tried to lighten the mood. "I'm honored to be your first stop," he said. "This moving on, is that why you're in London?"

"Well, my dad was English, so I spent my summers here," Jane replied.

"I'm terribly sorry," he said dryly. Jane smiled at his English sense of humor.

"I'm here for work," she confessed.

"Your profile said that you were a scientist?"

Jane winced. "How did that read again?" But the next voice Jane heard wasn't Richard's.

"Beautiful scientist seeks bubbly Brit for good times and possible long-term relationship," said Darcy Lewis, interrupting. Both Jane and Richard looked up to see the quirky brunette standing before them. Darcy didn't wait for introductions. She immediately reached out her hand to shake Richard's. "I'm Darcy," she said before turning to Jane and mouthing the words *He's cute* to her.

"What are you doing here?" Jane asked, embarrassed. It was bad enough that Darcy put her up to this; it was even worse that she was crashing her blind date.

Darcy pulled up a chair, took a piece of bread from the basket on their table, then began to butter it with Richard's knife. "So, I show up to work at your lab-slash-girl cave, expecting you to be moping around in your pajamas—"

"There really needs to be a point to this!" Jane quickly said, cutting Darcy off.

"You know all that scientific equipment you don't look at anymore?" Darcy said in between bites. "You might want to start."

Darcy reached into her bag and pulled out Jane's phase meter. The needle on the device was still spiking and a wave of curiosity flashed in Jane's eyes. "It kind of looks like the reading Selvig was rambling about," Darcy continued. Then she turned to Richard to explain just who Selvig was. "Our friend. Brilliant scientist," she said, nonchalantly. "Kinda went crazy."

Jane had had enough and shot Darcy an evil look. "You need to go now."

Darcy sat at the table and stared at them both before finally rising to her feet. "I give you five minutes," she said to Jane. Then she turned to Richard and said, "She's great, huh?" Richard smiled. Then Darcy smiled. She reached down, grabbed the rest of the bread, and walked out of the restaurant.

Richard and Jane stared at one another in disbelief. "So . . . why are you in London?" Jane finally asked, trying desperately to bring herself back to the table with Richard. But it was no use. Darcy was right. Jane couldn't stay at lunch. She had to get out of there. She had to check the phase meter and calculate the coordinates of the spike. She had to find Thor!

In less than five minutes, Jane was sliding into the passenger seat of the red sedan that was idling outside the restaurant. Darcy was behind the wheel, and someone Jane didn't know was in the backseat.

"Did you bring the butter?" the English college kid in the backseat asked.

Jane turned to the lanky guy in the backseat. "Who are you?" she asked.

"He's my intern," Darcy said with pride. "He's free."

"It's a great honor to be working with you, Dr. Foster," the intern said. Jane was taken aback, then decided to accept the situation and handed him the phase meter.

"Okay, intern. Find this!" she said. The kid looked at the coordinates and gave Darcy directions. Their car drove wildly through the streets of London, much to the dismay of other drivers, pedestrians, and even pigeons.

"I've totally mastered London driving," Darcy said with complete satisfaction as she continued to endanger anyone, and anything, that might be on the street or in her path.

As they drove closer and closer to their unknown

destination, Jane tried to call Erik Selvig once more. "Erik, it's me again. Where are you? I flew here because you said you were on to something, and then you just vanished." Jane's tone grew more serious with every word. "You have to call us back. I think I found what you found."

Jane was worried about her friend. He hadn't returned any of their calls in six months, and deep down, she was concerned that he still might be under the influence of Thor's evil brother, Loki, who had manipulated Selvig's mind in an attempt to take over the world. Thor and the Avengers saved Selvig—and the world—but perhaps Selvig was still suffering the aftereffects.

"Straight ahead, one hundred meters!" the intern yelled from the backseat as the car careened through the narrow London streets.

"Maybe he's in the bathroom?" Darcy said in reference to Selvig. She turned to look at Jane, unaware that she was driving them directly toward a brick wall.

"Sixty meters . . . forty . . . twenty . . ." the intern continued from the back, also unaware of the impending impact.

"Darcy!" Jane yelled. Darcy whipped her head around and jammed on the brakes. The car stopped just in time—mere inches from the brick wall. They got out, lucky to have survived the ride, and looked around.

"Which way, intern?" Jane asked the college kid whom she had just met.

"This way. And it's Ian," he said.

"Lead the way, Ian," Jane replied, following him. Darcy looked from them, to the building, then back to them again.

"How come these things never happen in a nice park?" she asked. "I like parks."

The three of them continued forward, following the beeping of the phase meter. They were at their destination: an abandoned industrial complex in London's south side.

PART TWO

CHAPTER FOUR

JANE, DARCY, AND IAN slowly made their way through the gray, decaying industrial complex. Holding the phase meter out in front of them, they used it as their guide to locate whatever it was they were searching for.

As they passed through one set of large loading doors, Jane looked in to see metal shipping containers stacked end over end, like a child's building blocks. The sight reminded her of Stonehenge. The comparison of the two, and the mysteries they both held, was not lost on Jane. They were definitely in the right spot.

The three of them continued through the complex, passing the shattered window with the suspended glass and the puddle on the ceiling, until they heard tiny footsteps in the distance. Two shadowy figures emerged from the door opposite them. Darcy froze, momentarily freaked out by everything going on. But as the figures got closer, they saw that they were just children. It was Maddie and Navid.

"Are you the police?" Maddie asked.

"No, we are scientists," Jane began. "Well, I am," she said, looking over to both Darcy and Ian and giving them both a shrug.

"Don't tell them!" Navid said to Maddie in Farsi. "They'll make it go away!"

Jane and Ian looked at each other in confusion. They didn't speak this language, so they were at a loss as to what the kids were saying.

"Make what go away?" Darcy said to everyone's shock and surprise. No one could believe that she understood Farsi!

"What? I got skills," Darcy said, only slightly offended. "They are worried we are going to make something go away."

Jane looked from Darcy to the kids, then bent down on one knee to speak to them. "Can you show me?"

Maddie looked from Jane to Navid, then bent down and picked up a brick. She cocked her arm, about to fling the brick at the three grown-ups.

"Violence never solved anything!" Ian yelled, clearly afraid. But that didn't stop Maddie. She hurled the brick at full force and the three grown-ups ducked, but nothing happened. When they looked up, they saw the brick hovering in midair. Jane, Darcy, and Ian looked at one another in complete disbelief.

"That doesn't seem right," Darcy said, breaking the tension. It wasn't right. And Jane was determined to find out why.

Jane, Darcy, and Ian followed the kids through the complex and up a winding staircase to the next amazing discovery. Standing at the top of the staircase, Navid dropped a bottle down the shaft, but instead of hitting the ground, it disappeared in midair halfway down. Everyone was stunned yet again, but when the bottle then reappeared at the top of the staircase, then fell, disappeared, and reappeared again—only faster this time—they were shocked even more.

Amazed, Jane had to try it for herself. She picked up a soda can and threw it. Like the bottle, it too disappeared, but unlike the bottle, Jane's soda can never reappeared. "Sometimes they come back, sometimes they don't," Navid said very matter-of-factly.

"I want to do it," Darcy said with excitement. "Jane, give me your shoe!" But Jane ignored Darcy and instead rushed off, following the direction of the now-intense beeping of the phase meter. She hadn't seen readings like this since New Mexico. Since Thor.

CHAPTER FIVE

THE MAJESTIC realm of Asgard, with its flowing rivers, ornate towers, and massive gold observatory, seemed to hover within the cosmos, as if magically suspended among the sparkling stars and rotating planets.

In the center of this beautiful land was its most iconic and important structure—the palace of King Odin Allfather, ruler of Asgard, and his wife, Queen Frigga. Beneath the enormous throne room, the large and lively dining rooms, the calming healing room, and the rest, lay the Asgardian dungeon. Located at the very most bottom level of the palace—lower still than the heavily guarded vault room that housed Asgard's most amazing and dangerous treasures—the dungeon was a dark, dank, and nearly inescapable structure that was home to some of the worst criminals, thieves, and murderers in the Nine Realms of the cosmos. And today, its occupancy was about to increase. The royal Einherjar escorted the captured Marauders to their individual cells, all of which were sealed with an impenetrable bluish energy barrier.

Watching the proceedings from his own inescapable cell was Loki, adoptive son of Odin and Frigga, and stepbrother to Thor. For crimes against both Asgard and Earth, Loki was held as a prisoner in the bowels of his own home, locked away, for all eternity. Looking out at the hopeless Marauders, Loki turned and spoke. "Odin continues to bring new friends. How thoughtful."

But Loki wasn't talking to himself; he was talking to his visitor, the only visitor he ever got—his mother,

Queen Frigga. The queen made a point to visit her son, and to bring him some amenities from his old life, like his collection of books. But they all sat unopened and untouched in a dark corner of his cell. "The books I sent . . . do they not interest you?" Frigga asked.

"Is that what I am supposed to do while away for eternity? Reading?" Loki replied in disgust.

"I have done everything in my power to make you comfortable, Loki," the queen responded.

"And does Odin share your concern?" Loki began, slowly moving toward his mother. "Or Thor? It must be inconvenient, my brother asking after me day and night," he said with sarcasm in his voice.

"You know full well it was *your* actions that brought you here," Frigga said. This only angered Loki further.

"I was merely given truth to the lie I've been told my entire life: that I was born to be a king," Loki stated as a matter of fact.

"A true king admits his faults. You have yet to take

responsibility for any of your choices." Frigga asked, her anger escalating, "What of the lives you took on Earth?"

"A mere handful compared to the number Odin has taken himself," Loki said with a vicious smile.

"Your father—"

"He is not my father!" Loki yelled, his voice echoing throughout the chamber.

There was a moment of silence, and then Frigga finally spoke. "Then am *I* not your mother?" she whispered.

"You are not," Loki said, his words stabbing.

"Always so perceptive about everyone but yourself," Frigga said as Loki reached his hand up to hers. But Loki's hand merely moved through her, and with a shimmer, the image of Frigga dissolved into the ether.

Several stories above, inside her chamber, the real Frigga stood over a fire pit and watched as the image of Loki faded in the flames and smoke. "He will only disappoint you," a voice said from behind her, breaking her out of her trance. It was Thor.

"Why indulge him?" Thor continued. "The gifts? The visits?" Thor couldn't understand how Frigga still had so much compassion for someone who had done so much evil.

"I think if you ask the guards, they will tell you I was never there," Frigga said with a hint of smile. She made her way over to Thor and continued. "What would you have me do? I am his mother and he is my son. I loved you no less when you were banished."

"Our crimes were hardly equal," Thor was quick to point out. Then he added, "Don't you ever regret teaching him your magic?"

"You and your father cast long shadows," Frigga began, hoping to finally make Thor understand. "I had hoped that by sharing my gifts with Loki, he could feel some sun for himself."

"But you were wrong."

"For the moment."

"You still see good in him, don't you?" Thor asked.

"I see glimmers of light I thought long extinguished," Frigga stated, optimistic that Thor might one day share her point of view.

Thor lowered his head. "Loki forfeited my forgiveness long ago." The two stood opposite each other for a long, silent moment, until Frigga decided it best to change the subject.

"Am I to take it by your presence that the Nine Realms still stand?"

"I came to give father the good news," Thor said, his smile returning.

"And you thought to find him here? You'll find him where he is more at ease," she said. Thor should've known. Odin wouldn't be in the palace at a time like this. He'd be with his men. Training.

Heavy broadswords clashed against shields, spears were thrown at high velocity toward their targets, and armored guards battled against one another in elaborate war games. Lead by Tyr, the Einherjar drill instructor known for the metal hand that replaced the real one that he had lost long ago in glorious battle, these were the Asgardian training grounds, and they were very, very active. Above it all circled two large black ravens. They watched the proceedings with keen interest before landing on a ledge next to the King of Asgard, Odin Allfather, who looked down at his troops. While still a great sovereign leader, Odin was growing older, and with age came the fatigue and weariness that only ruling can bring.

Thor approached his father with news that Vanaheim was finally secure. Odin was relieved that the Nine Realms were safe, but also felt the constant burden of always having to be the one to protect them. "For the first time since the Bifrost was destroyed, the Nine Realms are at peace, well reminded of our strength. You have earned their respect, and my gratitude," he told his son. But he could sense that something was wrong.

"I felt something on Vanaheim," Thor said. "A presence . . . a darkness . . ."

"And you would like to investigate?" Odin asked. "On Earth, perhaps?" Odin continued, wondering if this was really a ploy for Thor to return to Midgard. They had had this conversation before.

"This isn't about Jane Foster," Thor began, "though I have pledged to protect her realm. If something is amiss in the universe—"

Odin cut him off. He was tired of this conversation. "Nothing is amiss. Save your distracted heart," he instructed. "Mortal lives are fleeting. You would be better served by what lies in front of you," Odin said, nodding down at the training grounds, and at the arrival of Lady Sif, who was instructing the Einherjar on how to disarm an opponent. Feeling like she was being watched, Sif looked up and caught Thor's eye.

AFTER THOUSANDS OF YEARS in slumber, an ancient race of Dark Elves, led by their leader Malekith, have awoken.

With the **CONVERGENCE** dawning on the universe, strange occurrences begin on Earth.

All is quiet on the forest planet of Vanaheim until space pirates known as MARAUDERS suddenly attack a nearby Vanir campground!

The Bifrost opens and out steps the Warrior of Asgard, Thor! He unleashes a shockwave using his mythical hammer MJOLNIR!

THE MIGHTY THOR and the Asgardian soldiers, the Einherjar, battle the Marauders.

While his brother is off saving the universe, LOKI reads inside his prison cell located under the royal palace.

Thor returns to Asgard to inform his father, KING ODIN, that he has brought peace back to the Nine Realms.

But Thor and Odin are unaware that after thousands of years, the DARK ELVES have returned to take back what they think is rightfully theirs: The Universe!

When Thor learns that JANE FOSTER has come in contact with a dark energy, he travels to Earth to find and protect her.

Realizing the best place for Jane to be is by his side, Thor takes her to ASGARD, where she meets his royal family and friends.

When the Dark Elf leader, Malekith, and his army invade Asgard,
FRIGGA wields a sword and prepares to protect the earthling.

With his trusty spear GUNGNIR by his side, Odin Allfather lays
waste to over a dozen invading Dark Elves.

With the palace in shambles, MALEKITH is one step closer to destroying Odin . . . and Asgard.

Now that he has had his revenge on Asgard, Malekith leaves for his next target: EARTH!

As Thor surveys the damage done by Malekith and his army, he vows to SEEK REVENGE.

The two smiled at one another as Odin continued. "I tell you this not as your Allfather, but as your father: Lament not what you have lost"—looking toward Lady Sif, he continued—"but embrace what you have won."

Thor thought heavily. His heart was still on Midgard, with Jane, but he would consider his father's words.

"Now go," Odin continued. "Join your warriors. Revel in their celebration. At the very least enjoy yourself."

Thor bowed to his father. "We shall drink Asgard dry."

CHAPTER SIX

ON THE DECREPIT, decaying world of Svartalfheim, the air was poisonous to the Dark Elves. With their expressionless helmets covering their faces, an army of Dark Elves marched in formation along a jagged cliff side, until one elf raised a weapon and fired. It was the same type of black hole–inducing device that the scouts had used, and in a matter of seconds, the cliff imploded in on itself, sucking itself into a newly created miniature black hole. The elf stood stoic, and then continued to lead them on.

Meanwhile, deep within the catacombs, more elves fired even more devices, which caused even more miniature black holes to form and suck away the rocky terrain. The elf minions were training for battle and preparing for war.

On the cliff above, Algrim approached Malekith, who was standing without his helmet, rasping as he breathed in the toxic air. "My wife and I would sit here on the shore and watch our children play. I can still see the reflection of the waves on her face and feel the cool of the black wind," Malekith said as he kneeled down and sifted through black ash that covered the land. "I will restore our world to its former splendor or I will breathe this poison air until it kills me."

In a show of support, Algrim unhooked and removed his mask, and breathed in the same toxic air. Malekith was impressed by his fellow Dark Elf's loyalty. Algrim hid his pain and began to speak. "The scouts bring word from Vanaheim. The Asgardians are taking prisoners," he said.

"Prisoners? Time has made them weak." Then Malekith pointed toward his men and looked to Algrim. He didn't even have to say the words to his second in command.

"We are making progress," Algrim informed his master. He would make sure that the elves trained until they were ready. This was a fight that they were not prepared to lose.

"Good. Soon the Asgardians will know our pain as their own," Malekith said, looking out at dozens of Dark Elf Ark spaceships, all of which had crashed on this planet more than a thousand years ago, all of which served as a grim reminder of what the Dark Elves had lost, and just who was responsible.

PART THREE

CHAPTER SEVEN

THE CELEBRATION had been going on strong for the last few hours, and there wasn't an end in sight. Asgardians strolled through the streets, rejoicing the fact that the Nine Realms were safe at last.

Friends laughed, kids played, and warriors recounted their many victorious battles. At one particular pub, Thor and the Warriors Three were holding court, with Volstagg as the master of ceremonies—and the master storyteller—even if his stories tended to be somewhat exaggerated and partly fabricated. Still, his yarns kept everyone entertained, particularly his wife and children, who were on the edge of their seats, waiting to hear how they escaped the latest death-trap and insurmountable odds. Across the room, Fandral sat with a bar wench on each arm, while Thor stood in the background, alone but amused.

"I threw the beast off, but six more beat me to the ground, crushing my sword as if it were paper!" Volstagg continued to the captive group. His children jumped onto his lap to hear the story's big dramatic ending, and momentarily distracted him. "Where was I?" he suddenly stopped and asked.

"You were surrounded," Thor answered.

"By the most vile criminals the Nine Realms had ever produced," Volstagg continued, without missing a beat. "One thousand strong marched upon us!"

"One thousand?" Fandral quietly questioned to Thor.

Thor smiled at Volstagg's elaboration. "One thousand each," he said to Fandral, kidding.

"And who was there to face this horde but Fandral

the Dashing, Hogun the Grim, and Volstagg the—"

"—Voluminous!" a wench yelled from across the table.

"Fat!" Fandral immediately corrected.

"Invincible!" Volstagg stated. "To our left, savage beasts. Their fangs like knives!" he said, scaring the young children. "To our right, soldiers of fortune, blood dripping from their blades. I don't mind telling you, I feared for Thor's life." Thor raised an eyebrow, surprised at where this story was headed.

"But with steely courage, inspired spirit, and an ax . . ." Volstagg said as he slammed his battle-ax onto the table. The kids jumped as the ax sank into the wood and stuck out of the tabletop. "Victory was ours!" Volstagg yelled, ending this story to the cheer of the crowd.

"Truly a tale for the ages," Thor remarked with a smirk.

"By the time the night is through, we'll have defeated Surtur himself," Fandral said, referring to the fire demon from Muspelheim, who was one of the most heinous enemies of Thor and the Warriors Three.

Thor watched as Volstagg kissed his wife and cuddled with his children before beginning his next story. He then looked over at Fandral, who now had three giggling maidens at his side. Trying to revive his old enthusiasm, Thor threw his stein to the ground and yelled for another. There was a roar from the crowd as they did the same. With everyone cheering and drinking, Thor quietly made his way to the exit.

"There was a time when you would celebrate for a week," a voice said from behind him. It was Lady Sif. She smiled at Thor, and he smiled back. "There was a time when every battle came down to us, you and me, back to back, fighting for each other." Sif took a long drink and watched Thor's smile fade. "Stay. We will celebrate like old times. Surely the Allfather will have no further tasks for you tonight," Sif said. But Thor was in no mood for celebrating.

"This is one I set for myself," Thor told her. And without saying the words, Sif knew just who and what Thor was talking about.

"There are more than Nine Realms," she said. "The future king must focus on more than one."

"I have always been grateful for your words and your counsel, Lady Sif." And with that, Thor turned and walked off into the cool Asgardian night, alone.

Back on Earth, in the abandoned industrial complex in London, Darcy, Ian, Maddie, and Navid were playing a game of Disappearing Shoes. They would find whatever object they could—be it bottles, shoes, or even car keys—and throw them into the void, waiting to see which ones returned and which ones disappeared.

"Were those our car keys?" Darcy asked after Ian's latest throw.

"Maybe," he sheepishly replied. They were, and unfortunately, they never reappeared.

And while the interns and the kids played, Jane continued on through the complex, her phase meter pinging wildly as she searched for clues.

At that same time, back on Asgard, Heimdall, the all-seeing keeper of the Rainbow Bridge, stood at his post at the edge of the observatory, scanning the cosmos. He did not turn when Thor approached, but spoke as soon as the prince was behind him. "You are not celebrating," Heimdall said.

"Merriment can sometimes be a heavier burden than battle," Thor replied.

"Than you are doing one of them incorrectly," Heimdall observed. Thor couldn't help but smile.

"How fare the stars?" Thor asked. "Let me guess: shining?"

"Play the fool all you like," Heimdall began. "But when I taught you of the cosmos as a boy, you hung on my every word. Do you recall what you learned of the Convergence?" the sentry asked.

Thor remembered a little of its history. "The alignment of worlds . . . it approaches?" Thor asked.

"The universe has not been host to this marvel since before my watch began," Heimdall replied. Thor thought back to the darkness he felt on Vanaheim.

"Have you noticed anything strange?" he asked.

"From here, I can see Nine Realms and ten trillion souls. You don't know the meaning of the word strange," Heimdall replied. Thor would have to be more specific.

"On our last campaign, I sensed something. We had won our battle, but a greater turmoil lay just outside my sight," Thor explained.

Try as he might, Heimdall could not see any disturbances. But Thor did not take his leave. There was something else on his mind, and he knew that

Heimdall knew why he was really there—but Heimdall was going to make Thor ask.

Finally, after several long seconds of awkward silence, Thor gave in.

"How is she?" Thor said at last.

Heimdall turned his gaze toward Midgard, then finally responded. "She is well. She studies the Convergence as you once did. Even as we speak, she nears the truth."

CHAPTER EIGHT

JANE FOSTER was nearer to discovering the truth than either she or Heimdall could have ever thought. As she followed her pinging phase meter, she found herself at a doorway. Curious, Jane looked inside to see a shimmering rift in time and space. "Amazing . . ." she muttered to herself. And then things went really crazy.

Jane's shoes squeaked on the floor, and she found herself being dragged toward the rift as if by some all-powerful, invisible force. Jane reached out to grab hold of something—anything—but it was no use. Everything in the room was being pulled toward its center, toward a swirling gravitational darkness. She tried to yell for Darcy, but it was no use. By the time she opened her mouth to scream, she was consumed by the dark, swirling energy. The only sound was the wind whipping by her and the crackling of energy. The force lifted Jane high into the air and she hung, weightless, suspended above the ground. Then she started to spin with the rest of the debris. As with the soccer ball, the shoes, and the keys, strange, other-worldly forces were at work, causing gravity to reverse itself and objects to move independently and at varying speeds. And in the center of it all was a shocked Jane Foster. The energy crackled louder and louder and Jane spun faster and faster until everything went black.

Jane hit the ground with a hard *THUMP*, as if she had fallen several stories. She groaned as she slowly pulled herself up. She was bruised and her body ached, but she was alive, and nothing was broken.

"Darcy? Intern guy?" she called out, but there was no response. In a few seconds, her eyes became acclimated to the surrounding darkness.

Jane was lying on her side, in the dreary abandoned industrial complex on the south side of London. Confused, she tried to focus her eyes on what was directly above her on the ceiling—a large pile of bricks. As she slowly got to her feet, one of the bricks fell. Then Jane's eyes went wide as the entire pile fell. Jane jumped out of the way, just in time to miss being crushed by the mound of bricks. That was when it all came back to her: the odd occurrences at the complex, the strange phase readings, the dark room with the strange energy. She needed to find answers—and fast. But first she needed to find Darcy.

Meanwhile, Maddie and Navid continued to play with their magical soccer ball until, without warning, their soccer ball just bounced harmlessly off the side of the wall, its magic gone. The kids saw Jane enter the room, and thought that she had taken the magic away. "Now the police are going to kick us out," Navid said. "Thanks for nothing."

Jane looked out the window to see Darcy talking to a police officer, with several more behind her. Jane ran out of the complex as fast as she could.

"You called the police?" Jane yelled at Darcy, worried that they were going to make her evacuate the complex. "Next thing you know, S.H.I.E.L.D. will be crawling all over, 'Area Fifty-one-ing' the whole place!" Jane was frantic. "We had a stable gravitational anomaly. We had unprecedented success. Our only competition was kids!" she yelled.

"What was I supposed to do?" Darcy replied. "You were gone for five hours!" she yelled back.

This stopped Jane cold. How could that be? How did she disappear for five hours? She had only been in that strange room for a minute. Nothing was making sense, but before Jane could get any answers, storm clouds rolled in and the sky turned black. Darcy knew at once what this meant, but didn't want to believe it. "Really?" she said, as if to some higher power. And as if in response, the rain started.

Torrential rain poured down from the sky as everyone ran for cover, leaving Jane standing alone in the courtyard. She looked around, but somehow, she wasn't getting wet. She was staying dry. And that's when Jane realized what was happening. She heard a thunderclap and then, from behind, a large shadow engulfed her tiny one. She slowly turned and looked up to see Thor standing in all his glory, Mjolnir at his side, his red cape flowing in the wind. He was here. And he was real. He walked up to her, the two now in their own small, dry oasis.

"Are you all right?" Thor asked with concern. "I thought something had—"

SLAP! Jane hit Thor across the face.

"I just wanted to make sure you were real," she

said in reference to the slap. Thor just blinked, surprised and slightly annoyed at the reaction to his arrival. "Where were you?" Jane asked.

"Where were *you?*" Thor replied.

"Right where you left me," Jane said, referring to New Mexico.

"No," Thor interrupted. "Heimdall could not see you. You were gone."

Jane looked down and realized what Thor meant. "I don't know what— Wait, Heimdall was watching me?" she asked.

"He was always watching you. I asked him to," Thor said.

"I need a moment to figure out if that's moving or creepy," Jane replied, though deep down she knew what Thor meant. "I waited for you," she confessed.

"I know you did," Thor began.

"You said you'd come back for me," Jane said with sadness, wondering why Thor never did.

"The Bifrost was destroyed. The Nine Realms fell

into chaos. Entire planets and people were at risk," Thor explained. "Risk of destruction. It was my obligation to help them."

"But I saw you on TV," Jane said. "In New York."

"My duty had to take precedence over my heart," Thor said, referring to his battle with the Avengers against Loki.

Jane smiled at Thor, but was interrupted by Darcy, who stood outside their oasis, soaking wet. "Do you wanna, maybe . . . ?" Seeing her, Thor stopped the rain. Jane looked over at the police, who were arresting Ian, and ran over to try to explain, leaving Darcy alone with Thor. "Look at you," Darcy said as she inspected Thor in his battle armor. "Still all muscle-y and stuff and everything. How's space?"

"Space is fine," Thor said, his eyes on Jane and the police. They had moved toward her now, as if to arrest her as well.

"This is private property," one officer began. "You're trespassing. The lot of you. You'll have to come down to the station." But as the bobby reached out to her, Thor took a step forward. As he did, the police reflexively drew their guns. The situation had gone from bad to worse in a matter of seconds.

"Place your hands on your head and take five steps back!" one of the officers yelled.

Thor protested that Jane was sick. He could tell that something was wrong, but the police did not back down.

Jane tried to calm him down, but was suddenly too weak to even stand. Thor contemplated for a moment, then kneeled down beside Jane. "Close your eyes," he instructed as he lifted her into his arms. Everything went silent. Then everything and anything that wasn't nailed down to the ground began to shake, and with a deafening *BOOM!* the Bifrost shot down to Earth and whisked Thor and Jane up into the sky.

Darcy and the police looked at each other as the giant beam of light disappeared. They were all speechless.

With a mighty flash of light, cinder blocks, parking meters, and car hoods emerged from the Bifrost, causing a nonplussed Heimdall to move out of the way to avoid being hit from the debris that was accidentally sucked into the wormhole. With another flash, Thor and Jane landed in the observatory. Upon seeing them, Heimdall removed his sword from the controls, causing the observatory to stop spinning and the Bifrost to close.

Jane staggered to her feet as Thor reached out to steady her and make sure that she was all right. Jane looked up at him and grinned like a giddy schoolgirl. "We have to do that again!" she said with a smile.

Across the cosmos, Malekith strode through Svartalfheim, seething with rage. He could not wait to make the Asgardians pay for their injustice to him, his world, and his people. As the Dark Elf leader neared the Ark spaceship Algrim approached, struggling to keep up. When the two were out of earshot of the rest of the elves, Malekith began to speak. He instructed Algrim to take on a top secret plan that only he could accomplish. The second in command slowly nodded his acceptance. Malekith placed a reassuring, thankful hand on Algrim's shoulder, then turned and looked out upon his awaiting army. They were falling into formation outside the large Ark. The war with Asgard was about to begin anew.

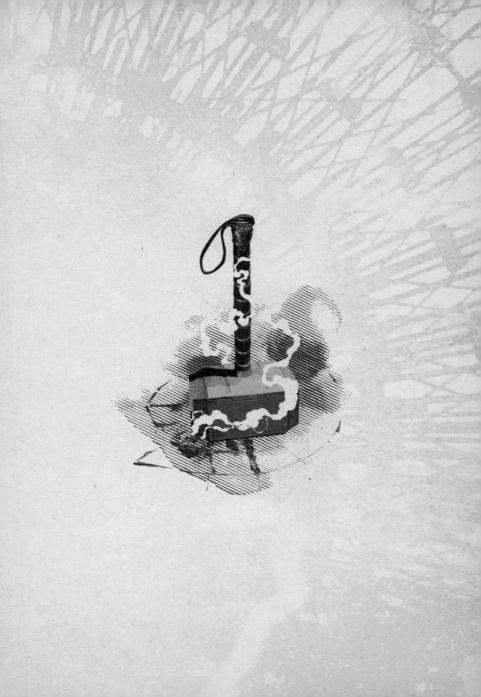

CHAPTER NINE

THOR STOOD BY, waiting and worried, as Eir, goddess of healing, examined Jane inside the palace's healing room. As Jane was from another realm, Thor wanted her to get a thorough scanning from Eir, just to make sure the trip to Agsard would not affect her. Rather than lie still, Jane reached out to touch all of the new technology around her and asked questions about any new device she saw. This caused Eir to get a bit frustrated with Jane. Thor reached out and held Jane's hand to distract her long enough for Eir to continue her examination.

Eir moved a Soul Forge—a small crystalline

device—over Jane's body. The device projected an image of Jane's insides overhead, as if it were a holographic X-ray of some sort. Just as Jane was about to ask a question about the strange device, Odin burst into the room, flanked by two Einherjar.

Holding Gungnir, which was both his battle spear and royal scepter, Odin glared at Thor, barely able to contain his rage. "Are my words mere noises to you, that you ignore them completely?" the Allfather yelled.

"She is ill," Thor began, before Odin cut him off.

"She is mortal! Illness is their defining trait. She no more belongs in Asgard than a goat at a table," Odin said. This got Jane's attention.

"Excuse me, who are you?" she asked, weak but still strong enough to put up a fight.

"I am Odin, King of Asgard and protector of the Nine Realms," he stated. Jane began to introduce herself, but he cut her off, too. "I know who you are," Odin said, clearly unhappy with them both.

"Father, I think something has happened to her,"

Thor said. "Something I cannot explain."

"Her world has its healers. They can deal with it," Odin said. Then he turned to the two Einherjar. "Return her to Midgard," he instructed. But as one guard reached out for her, Eir intervened.

The healer pointed to the hologram. The Asgardian sensed something was not right with the earthling's biological readings.

Odin looked from Eir to Jane, then moved Gungnir over Jane's body. He stepped back and sighed. Instantly, the Allfather knew that Thor was right: Jane would be safer on Asgard than Midgard. She wasn't going anywhere.

Thor and Jane followed Odin through the palace to the Hall of Science. Jane looked around, awestruck. In the center of the room was Yggdrasil, the tree of life. Asgardians circled the tree, passing their hands through holographic pillars of light that showed images and gave information. Jane's curiosity got the best of her, and she reached into the light, the rays falling over her fingers like water. Suddenly, there was a loud *BONG!* It was a sound unlike anything Jane had ever heard before, and it rang throughout the Hall of Science. Everyone within the hall stopped and turned to stare at the earthling. Lowering her head to hide her embarrassment, Jane quickly realized that the sound meant *Don't touch.* She quietly folded her hands behind her back and walked with Thor.

"Some believe that before the universe, there was nothing," the Allfather said as they entered the palace library. "They are wrong." Odin lifted a huge tome from the wall and brought it down in front of them. "Before the universe there was darkness, and woe betide the warrior that almost mistakes darkness for nothing."

Thor nodded to his father, an acknowledgement of the Allfather's unspoken apology.

"The Nine Realms are not eternal," Odin continued. "They have a dawn just as they have a dusk. Before the dawn, the Dark Elves reigned unchallenged," Odin said as he leafed through the book. "But then came the birth of light. The darkness faded, revealing the Nine Realms as we know them." As Odin spoke, the book shone brightly, mirroring what the Allfather was explaining.

Jane caught on quickly, and related the events to Earth science. "You're talking about the Big Bang, aren't you?" she asked.

"I am reading to you from the sacred, all-knowing record of our existence," Odin said, his tone growing more annoyed as he spoke. "Do you have something to add?"

Thor shot Jane another look, then spoke up. "You'll find Jane knows of what you speak . . . and often speaks of what she knows." Jane understood Thor's unspoken warning, and spoke up to explain.

"We have a theory on Earth," Jane started.

"Fourteen billion years ago, a high-energy density led to a rapid expansion of particles. A massive explosion occurred, then cooled into what we now call the universe." She gave Odin an apology in the form of a smile. "The Big Bang," she said.

Odin continued. "The birth of light changed the very nature of the universe. The Dark Elves resisted. Their leader, Malekith, built a weapon out of the darkness and waged war against the Nine Realms." Odin turned the page and the book showed Malekith leading an army of Dark Elves. "After years of bloodshed, my father, Bor, finally triumphed. He offered the Dark Elves a truce. But Malekith would not live in a universe he could not rule."

Jane looked at Thor, nervous, then back to Odin. It was going to be a long night. . . .

At dawn the next morning, Heimdall opened the Bifrost to let Lady Sif, Fandral, and Volstagg reenter Asgard. They were with a battalion of Einherjar, and they had with them another group of chained alien prisoners. "When, exactly, did we become the prison of the Nine Realms?" Sif asked upon her return.

"At times of chaos, it is best to keep your enemies close at hand," Heimdall said as he deactivated the controls. As the observatory stopped spinning, Volstagg and Fandral escorted the prisoners toward the dungeons beneath the palace. Volstagg couldn't help but agree with Sif.

"Acting as caretaker to these scoundrels is beneath us," he said.

"If they were beneath you, they'd be dead!" Fandral joked.

Meanwhile, across the realm, inside her own chambers within the palace, stood Jane. She was amazed. The architecture was traditional and ornate, but also modern and futuristic, and in the center of the room was a fire pit in which multicolored flames danced. Jane was suitably impressed.

"Thor wanted you to have the best room in the palace," Eir said as she showed Jane inside. "Your continued health is of the utmost importance to him." Jane continued to look around the room and noticed an assortment of elegant gowns and dresses.

"And the dresses?" Jane asked as Eir walked toward the door. "Do they have some kind of medical value?"

"They don't hurt," Eir said as she closed the door. Jane looked around the room. Even her dreams weren't this good. Maybe things were finally looking up.

Far below Jane's chambers, inside the dungeon, a Marauder slammed his fist against his cell's energy barrier. The impact shocked him, and threw him across his cell. There was no escape. This was true for every prisoner in the dungeon. But once Malekith's plan unfolded, all of that would change. . . .

Aboveground, on one of Asgard's many splendid plazas, stood Thor. He was searching for Jane, who finally arrived. She was dressed in a stunning Asgardian gown, and she looked beautiful. In her hand was a golden sphere. As she approached Thor, she threw the sphere into the air. It burst into a dozen parts, hovered for a second, then reformed into a perfect sphere. Jane was awestruck. "This is amazing. The magnetic propulsion alone would advance Earth's by decades," she said with excitement. "If I could get this to a lab, I could determine—" But Thor cut her off. Then he pointed to a group of children staring at her from the other side of the plaza.

"You have their ball," he said as he nodded toward

the kids. Embarrassed, Jane handed the ball to the children, who were now laughing at the situation. Jane quietly made her way to Thor.

"The gown suits you," he said upon her return.

"I feel like I'm going to the prom," she said. "Though hopefully this time, I won't come back from the bathroom and find my date making out with Heather Abramowitz."

Thor was confused. "Should this Heather Abramowitz appear, she shall answer to me," he said.

Jane smiled at him and the two began to stroll through the plaza, unaware that danger lurked beneath their feet.

"My father would've given anything to see this," Jane told Thor as she thought about her dad.

"He was a scientist too?" Thor wondered.

"Yes, at Cambridge. He was British; my mom was American. They were from different worlds. Relatively speaking," she said, painfully aware how she and

Thor were *literally* from different worlds.

As they continued on, Jane began to question him about why Heimdall couldn't see her for a period of time. Thor believed that Jane might not have been entirely on Earth when the dark energy swirled around her in London. Jane didn't see how this was possible, so Thor began to explain the Convergence to her.

"The Nine Realms travel within Yggdrasil, orbiting Midgard, much like the way our planets orbit the sun," he began. "Every five thousand years, the realms align. This is called the Convergence. During that time, the borders between the realms become soft. It is possible you found one of these points," he said. "We are lucky it remained open. Once the realms are out of alignment, no science can reopen the door."

"You never know," Jane said to him, smiling. "Science could surprise you."

Thor lifted her hand and kissed it.

"I will find a way to make sure it does," he said.

"Your father said there wasn't one," Jane replied, referring to Odin's feelings on science.

"My father does not know everything," Thor said, but just as he did, he heard a different voice call out to him from behind them.

"Don't let him hear you say that," the voice said. Thor froze, then turned to see Queen Frigga staring at them, a sly smile on her face.

"Mother!" Thor said with surprise.

Jane shot him a look—she wasn't prepared to meet his mother! She quickly pulled her hand away.

"I was just out shopping for dinner," Frigga said, but her ruse did not work on Thor.

"You have more than two hundred chefs," he said. This time, Frigga shot Thor a stern look. Thor sighed and realized he was outmatched.

"Jane Foster, this is my mother, Frigga, Queen of Asgard," Thor said. "Mother . . . this is Jane."

Frigga approached and took Jane's hand in hers.

"We have so much to talk about," Frigga said as she led Jane away.

Thor didn't like the looks of this. . . .

Back in the dungeon, it was time for Malekith's plan of destruction to be put into action. As dozens of hopeless Marauders sat in their cells, a blinding explosion rang out from one end of the dungeon. Debris and brick flew everywhere, and when the dust settled, a huge monster known as Kurse stood on top of the fallen dungeon wall. He snarled and roared and clenched his fists. Kurse looked around at the Marauders, who now stood at the end of their cells, just waiting to be freed so they could seek revenge on Asgard for locking them away. A smirk came across the beast's dark face as hope fell across the Marauders'. Kurse stepped to the first invisible energy barrier that housed a dozen of the prisoners. He pulled back his giant fist and unleashed a devastating blow, shutting down the force field. It flickered out, and the Marauders were free! Then Kurse began breaking and punching open cell after cell as waves of dangerous, and soon to be armed, prisoners raced up the stairs to confront Asgard.

As Kurse entered the dungeon's hallway, alarms began to sound. Hearing the commotion, two Einherjar rushed over to investigate. But Kurse was faster and stronger. Since he had already started to deactivate other cells, by the time the Einherjar arrived on the scene, it was already too late. Prisoners were running wild.

Kurse continued through the dungeon, freeing prisoners and lifting the weapons of defeated Einherjar who first came to the rescue. As Kurse walked through the dungeon, he suddenly felt a cold shimmer run down his spine. He stopped at one cell and peered in. Loki stared back. "The east stairs lead to the barracks. You'll find them mostly unguarded," Loki said. Kurse nodded, then continued on, glad for the inside information. Loki wanted revenge against Thor and Odin—he just hoped that he wasn't getting more than he hoped for. The fascination of Kurse stayed with Loki for a moment or two, then he returned to his books—which he was now reading.

Meanwhile, aboveground, Frigga and Jane walked and talked, while Thor trailed behind them, unaware of the horrors that were occurring several stories below his feet.

"I can't remember the last time Thor brought a friend home to meet us," Frigga said to Jane. "When a young man brings a young woman home to meet his parents . . ." Frigga began, implying a possible marriage between Thor and Jane.

"Technically, I think we have only known each other for three days," Jane said, surprised to be having this conversation so soon.

"And if it were three million, would that change how you feel?" Frigga asked.

Jane thought on this. It wouldn't change one thing.

Jane was about to respond when a horn blasted out in the distance. Thor and Frigga froze in their tracks as the horn blasted again.

"The prisoners—" Frigga gasped.

"Loki," Thor said with anger in his voice. The horns signaled a problem in the dungeons, and Thor feared that it was an escape attempt by his trickster brother, but he couldn't just leave Jane in the middle of Asgard unattended. Frigga realized this, too.

"Go. I will look after her," Frigga said, before both she and Jane added, "Be careful!" The two women looked at each other, worried about Thor.

Inside the dungeon, Volstagg and Fandral were battling against the escaped prisoners, trying valiantly to keep them within the confines of the dungeon. "It's as if they resent being imprisoned," Fandral cracked. A Marauder slammed into Fandral, knocking him down; then Volstagg did the same to the Marauder.

"There is no pleasing some creatures," Volstagg said with a smile, as he swung his battle-ax through the air, coming down on Marauder after Marauder. But his smile soon disappeared as a mob of escaped prisoners got the upper hand and surrounded the two warriors. Voltsagg and Fandral stood back-to-back, clearly outnumbered. Until . . .

THOOM! The Mighty Thor landed in front of his friends, Mjolnir down at his side. "Lay down your arms and return to your cells," Thor said. "You have my word, no harm will come to you."

A huge, menacing Marauder approached Thor, as if to surrender, then punched the Asgardian with a powerful blow, sending Thor back about an inch. Thor looked up, spit blood from his mouth, and gripped Mjolnir. "Very well. You do not have my word," he said, and in the blink of an eye, Thor raised his hammer and smashed the Marauder in the face, slamming him against a stone wall and knocking him out cold. Then with a roar, the prisoners charged Thor, Fandral, and Volstagg. The battle for Asgard had begun.

Across the realm, in Heimdall's observatory, the sentry turned his gaze toward the palace as the horns continued to blast. Heimdall grabbed his sword and began to run toward the palace to help, but something else caught his attention: it was the sound of wrenching metal and the churning of an engine, and it was coming from directly above him. Heimdall looked up to see the clouds warp in the sky. There was something hiding within them—something cloaked and unseen to all of Asgard. Unseen to all, except Heimdall. The mighty sentry quickly jumped onto the observatory's suspension cables and ran up the observatory, alongside the distortion in the sky. With all of his strength, Heimdall leaped into the air and landed on the invisible object. He then plunged his sword into it, causing the distortion to spark and, finally, reveal its true form: a Dark Elf Harrow ship. Heimdall raised his sword again and began slashing at the ship over and over, each strike more powerful and damaging than the last.

Heimdall's attack exposed the ship's gravity drive, and with another strike from his sword directly into the drive itself, the drive exploded, causing the ship to fall from the sky. Heimdall jumped to the safety of the observatory just as the ship crashed into the water.

The sentry allowed himself a moment of satisfaction as the ship sunk into the sea, but it was short-lived. Terror washed over Heimdall's face as the massive Ark ship and two more Harrows de-cloaked above the observatory and sped off toward the palace.

Inside the palace, Odin was strapping on his battle armor and preparing for war. He strode down a corridor and barked orders at Sif and a squad of elite Einherjar who followed behind. "Send a squadron to the weapons vault!" he ordered. "Defend it at all costs. Secure the dungeon!"

Just then, Frigga and Jane emerged from an adjoining corridor, and Odin immediately ordered his men to protect their queen. Sif eyed Jane suspiciously as Frigga looked at Odin with concern on her face.

"Just a skirmish," he said, lying. "Likely nothing to fear."

"Your eyes betray you," Frigga said to her husband. "They always have."

Odin smiled at his wife, then turned his attention

to Jane. "Take her to her chambers. I will come for you as soon as it's safe," Odin instructed.

"Take care," Frigga said to her king.

"Despite all I have survived, my queen still worries over me," Odin said as he touched her cheek gently.

"It's only because I have worried over you that you have survived," she replied. Odin gave her one last smile, then strode down the corridor with Sif close behind.

"You two have a very special relationship," Jane said to Frigga as she watched Odin leave.

"We trust each other," Frigga said as she grabbed a sword from one of the Einherjar and led Jane to her chambers.

Inside the palace throne room, there was a huge *CRASH!* As the smoke began to clear, Einherjar troops rushed inside to investigate, their swords drawn. A been blown off the wall and lay in pieces.

Einherjar moved closer to the dark hole in the wall but all they saw inside was blackness. Suddenly, tiny blasts emerged from the blackness, forming miniature black holes near the Einherjar. The guards were instantly sucked into the black holes, lost forever to the darkness.

The remaining Einherjar looked up, horrified. From the blackness of the hole, they saw twenty glowing yellow eyes peering out at them. All at once, the Dark Elves attacked with an unexpected ferocity. Savage and brutal, the Dark Elves cut down the Einherjar to make way for their leader. Malekith exited the ship and surveyed the scene, lifting a pistol and destroying Odin's throne.

Back in the dungeon, the battle was almost over. After nonstop fighting, Volstagg, Fandral, and Thor were down to the last few escapees. Volstagg smashed a Marauder into one of the brick walls, Fandral slashed at prisoners with his sword, and Thor slammed two

Marauders at once. As the last prisoner fell, the dungeon finally grew silent.

"How did they get out?" Fandral asked.

"Perhaps they can tell us," Thor said. "Round them up. One to a cell," he instructed.

But before the warriors could act, they heard a muffled explosion from above them. They looked to one another as the sounds of battle echoed once again through the dungeon. Then, turning to the side, they saw an Einherjar lieutenant rush toward them.

"Sire!" the guard yelled to Thor. "We are under attack! Dark creatures—I've never seen them before!"

Thor turned from the Einherjar and locked eyes with Loki, who sat motionless in his cell. Thor glared at his brother then shut down the energy barrier and entered his cell.

"What have you done?!" Thor yelled.

"Read, mostly. Pythagoras," he said. "Earlier I had a bowl of gruel," Loki said sarcastically. Thor stood mere inches from his brother's face, seething with explosions occurred aboveground, and ...anced upward. "Don't you think you ought to ...ok into that?" he said. Thor scowled at his brother, then strode off toward the stairs. Loki watched his brother leave, a hint of guilt in his eyes. What had he done?

Inside the palace, Malekith wiped out more and more Einherjar as he made his way toward Jane's chambers. The doors swung open and Malekith entered. Frigga raised her sword and stood her ground. "Stand down, creature, and you may still survive this," she ordered. In the background, Jane hid behind a heavy curtain near the balcony.

"I have survived worse, woman," Malekith said. He was out for revenge, and nothing was going to stop him, especially not her.

"Who are you?" Frigga replied, her sword still raised.

"I am Malekith, and I will have what is mine," the Dark Elf said as he made his way through her chambers. Frigga quickly spun around and swung her sword at Malekith's face, slashing him on his cheek. Malekith pulled his blade to strike back, but Frigga was too fast for him, and knocked Malekith's blade out of his hand. "You have a fine blade," Malekith said, genuinely impressed.

Frigga pressed forward, pointing her sword at Malekith's throat and pushing his back to the wall. "It's not the blade, but the woman who wields it," Frigga said.

Malekith smiled, then looked past her. Frigga turned, but she was too late. Kurse was already behind her, knocking the sword from her hand. Malekith moved between them and advanced toward Jane.

Malekith got closer to the earthling, and as he

lifted his blade, ready to strike, Odin and Sif burst into the room, surrounded by a phalanx of Einherjar.

Odin raised Gungnir and unleashed a massive burst of white energy, knocking everyone back. Malekith got to his feet as Kurse continued to hold on to Frigga, who struggled against the monster's massive strength.

"Your bravery will not ease your pain," Malekith replied threateningly.

"I've survived worse," Frigga said, repeating Malekith's own words back to him. But Odin had heard enough.

"Release her!" the Allfather yelled. He stamped Gungnir on the ground and it crackled with energy. "Release her or burn!" Odin screamed.

"Ah, the son of Bor," Malekith said. "I believe we have already met your queen," Malekith teased.

"I said release her, elf!" Odin demanded.

Malekith stared at Odin for what felt like an eternity. His time had finally come. A sour, sinister smile played around the corner of his lips. "Then you will face the same choice I did," Malekith said, momentarily reflecting on his own decisions. "What will it be, Asgardian? Your wife or your world?"

Frigga and Odin stared at one another. It was a no-win situation. Odin could not let Frigga die, but he also could not let Malekith have Asgard.

"What are you prepared to do for the people you love?" Malekith hissed.

As if in response, a huge thunderclap rang out, followed by a streak of lightning. Speeding through the palace was Mjolnir! The hammer smashed into Kurse with all its might, causing him to drop Frigga to the ground. It hung in midair a moment, then spun back to Thor, who was now standing in the doorway, angry and ready to fight.

Malekith lunged for Frigga, and Thor raised his hammer to the sky. He called down the lightning, which hit Mjolnir and then ricocheted off toward Malekith. The lightning bolt struck Malekith in the face, scarring him and knocking him down to the ground. As Frigga ran toward the safety of Odin and Thor, Kurse got to his feet and grabbed Malekith, who was still clutching his face in pain. The two Dark Elves then jumped off the balcony into the Asgardian sky. Thor raced to the balcony's edge, and saw the two elves land atop a waiting Harrow, which rushed off at full speed and disappeared into thin air. Thor raised his hammer to call down more lightning, but Odin steadied his son's hand. The enemy had escaped. The battle was over.

It was time to assess the damage. They had been attacked from within. Their defenses were down, and the palace was in ruins. Many Einherjar and innocent civilians now lay dead. It was time for the king and prince of Asgard to be with their people.

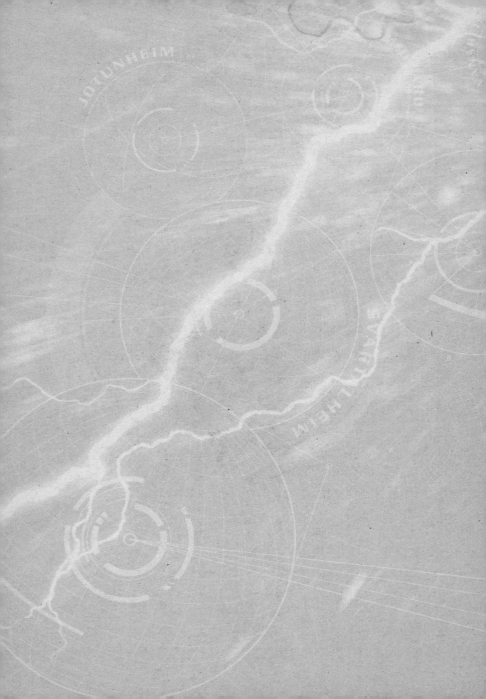

EPILOGUE

THE FUNERALS started the next day. Asgardians lined their rocky shoreline, each carrying a light that they would then release in honor of their fallen dead. Odin, Frigga, and Thor led the procession, followed by Sif, Volstagg, and Fandral.

"I like this not," Volstagg said. "War is not the time for public ceremonies. Or lights," the warrior said. But this was the Asgardian way. They would pay their respects for the ones they lost, then the battle would begin again. A battle for Asgard. And now that Jane Foster was involved, a battle for Earth.

In the back of the procession, among the surviving Einherjar, was Jane. She had all the eyes of Asgard upon her.

As the ceremony ended, Thor walked over to Jane, kissed her hand, and assured her that everything would be all right. He then moved away and spoke to Odin, Sif, and his fellow Asgardian warriors. Thor was forming a war council, and he was going to take the battle to Malekith, and all the way to Svartalfheim, if need be. The Dark Elves would not triumph, and Malekith would pay for his crimes. Thor swore this to himself, to his war council, and to the people of Asgard.

Thor spun his hammer faster and faster until he was rocketed up into the sky. He overlooked his home world and thought about what had happened and what was about to happen. Tomorrow a new fight would begin: a fight for Asgard, for Earth, and for the universe. And at its center would be the Mighty Thor.

Thor gripped Mjolnir and allowed a small smile

to come to his battle-worn face. It would be dangerous, but the battle would be glorious, and Thor would
not stop until he—and Asgard—were victorious. But
that is a tale for another day. . . .